CAPTAIN PE
PETS

SALLY GRINDLEY

Illustrated by
DAVID PARKINS

KING*f*ISHER

To Chris and Richard Downs – S.G.

To the staff and children of
St. Faith's Infant School, Lincoln – D.P.

KINGFISHER

An imprint of Kingfisher Publications Plc
New Penderel House, 283-288 High Holborn
London WC1V 7HZ

First published by Kingfisher 2002
2 4 6 8 10 9 7 5 3
TS1/1103/AJT/FR/115SMA

Text copyright © Sally Grindley 2002
Illustrations copyright © David Parkins 2002

A CIP catalogue record for this book
is available from the British Library.

ISBN 0 7534 0576 8

Printed in India

Contents

Chapter One

Captain Pepper wanted a pet –
but he didn't want a parrot.
"Every pirate I've ever
met has had a parrot,"
he said.
"Parrots talk too
much. No, I want
a pet that will
make me famous
all over the world."

"So let's go to the pet shop," said Pirate Nong.

"Goldfish are best," said Pirate Noodle.

"Let's buy a hamster!" said Pirate Noddypoll.

"Daft twits!" roared Captain Pepper.

"A hamster or a goldfish won't make
me famous! What I want is something
different."

What Captain Pepper wanted
Captain Pepper got.

So off they sailed, aboard the
Snooty Fox, to search for a pet
that was different.

Chapter Two

The pirates sailed for many long

weeks.

At last, they reached an island.

"Ah-ha!" cried
Captain Pepper.
"I'll bet my
boots we'll find
my pet here.
Full speed ahead,
you horrible lot!"

They sailed down a river and into
a jungle.

"Stop!" bellowed the Captain.

"Lower the gangplank and get ashore!
Find me a pet, or I'll feed you to the
sharks!"

Then Captain Pepper lay down
in his hammock for a nap.

"Come on," sighed
Pirate Nong.
"Let's find his pet,
then we can go home."

But as the pirates
stepped onto the gangplank
Noddypoll slipped . . .

and fell in the water.

"Help!" he screamed. "I can't swim!"

Suddenly, a huge toothy creature tossed
Noddypoll up in the air.

"Help!" he screamed. "I want my mum!"

Captain Pepper jumped
to his feet. "Bless my soul,
it's a hippopotamus!"
he shouted. "That
would make a good pet.
Bring it on board!"

The hippo didn't want
to be brought on board.
It snorted and stamped
and snapped at the
pirates.
But at last they
hauled it up
onto the deck.

CRASH!

The mast fell

onto the deck.

"Stop that now!" the Captain bellowed.

Captain Pepper glared at the hippo.

The hippo glared at Captain Pepper –

and charged!

Captain Pepper dived out of the way . . .

but the hippo kept going . . .

right over the side of the ship . . .

SPLASH!

and rushed across the ship.

CRUNCH!

It bit the mast in two.

"Welcome aboard, my hippo pet,"
said Captain Pepper.
"With you by my side, I'll soon be
famous all over the world."
He patted the hippo's head.

The hippo snorted . . .

"That hippo was trouble," said Pirate
Nong. "Can't we go home and buy
a parrot?"

Captain Pepper snorted and snarled.
"A parrot?" he roared. "Not on your
nelly! Find me something different,
or I'll feed you to the sharks!"

Chapter Three

The pirates set off into the jungle.

"The Captain should catch his own

pet," grumbled Noddypoll.

"Shhh!" said Nong.

"Look, by that tree! That's different."

A porcupine was scratching for grubs.

"It's black and white

like our pirate flag,"

said Nong.

"That would make a good pet for
Captain Pepper," said Noddypoll.
"Catch it, Noodle, before it runs off."
Noodle reached out his hand.

"Oww!" he squealed, and leapt in
the air. "Shiver me timbers!
It's covered in sharp things.
I'm not picking that up.
We'll find something else."
So on they went, tiptoeing slowly.

Suddenly, something hit Noddypoll on the head.

"Ouch!" he howled. "Who's throwing things?"

The pirates looked up into the trees.

The monkey threw another
nut, then it leapt to the
ground.

"That's different!" cried Nong.

"That would make a good
pet for Captain Pepper,"
said Noddypoll. "Catch it,
Noodle, before it runs off."

Noodle ran after the monkey, with
Noddypoll and Nong at his heels . . .

all the way back to the *Snooty Fox*.
"It's going on board!" said Noddypoll.

The pirates chased the monkey up the gangplank and onto the ship.

The monkey jumped on the Captain's hammock, and stole his hat.

Captain Pepper woke up from his nap.
"Stop!" he bellowed. "Give me back
my hat!"
The monkey climbed up the ropes
and swung on the sails.

"Get off my ship!" the Captain roared.

He waved his cutlass in the air.

SWISH! SWASH!

The monkey screeched and dropped the hat.
Then it ran down the gangplank and
disappeared back into the jungle.

"That monkey was trouble," said
Pirate Nong. "Can't we go home and
buy a parrot?"

Captain Pepper snorted and snarled.

"A parrot?" he roared. "Not on your nelly!
Find me something different, or I'll feed
you to the sharks!"

Chapter Four

It was getting dark when the pirates set off into the jungle again.

Noddypoll clung to Noodle and whimpered.

"Shhh!" said Nong. "Look, over there."

"A pussycat with spots! That's different," said Noddypoll.

"Catch it, Noodle, before it runs off."

"Here, Pussy," called Noodle.

"Come to Noodle, good Pussy."

The leopard crept

slowly towards him.

But the growl in its throat and the glint in its eye filled Noodle with fear.

"Shiver me timbers! He thinks I'm his dinner!" he cried.

Noodle turned and ran deeper into the jungle, with Noddypoll and Nong at his heels.

The jungle grew darker and even more scary.

On they went, tiptoeing slowly.

Then Noddypoll tripped over a fallen branch and landed on his bottom with a howl.

The branch began to wriggle.

"Aagh!" screamed Noddypoll.

"That branch is alive!"

"Well, shiver me timbers!" said Noodle.
"That's different!"

"Catch it, Noodle, before it runs off,"
said Noddypoll.

"It can't run," giggled Noodle.

"It's got no legs!"

He grabbed it by its middle and pulled.

"It's heavy," he cried. "You'll both

have to help."

Together, the pirates carried the snake
through the jungle and back to
the *Snooty Fox*.

Captain Pepper couldn't believe his eyes.
"A python! You've brought me
a python!" he cried.
He hopped and skipped across the deck.
"I'm going to be famous!" he whooped.

Then Captain Pepper clapped his hands
and began to sing:
"*O, a python is a wondrous thing,*
No arms, no legs has he.
And yet he moves with lightning speed
To catch and eat his tea."

"We've found you a pet," said Nong.

"Can we go home now, please?"

Captain Pepper stopped singing.

"Go home?" he roared. "Not on

your nelly! We're going round the

world to show off my python.

I'm going to be famous!"

The pirates grumbled behind his back.

"We'll be off at daybreak," said the

Captain. "So you'd better be ready,

or I'll feed you to the sharks!"

Chapter Five

Daybreak came.

The pirates slept peacefully in their
bunks.

At midday, Nong woke up and

stretched . . .

"Something
isn't right,"
he thought.

"Hey, wake up Noddypoll and
Noodle," he called. "It's late.
Why hasn't the Captain shouted at us?"
The pirates crept up on deck and
tiptoed towards Captain Pepper's
hammock.

There were the Captain's boots . . .

There was the Captain's hat . . .

but there was no sign of Captain Pepper.

In his place, fast asleep, was

Captain Pepper's python pet –

with a large bulge in its middle.

"Where's the Captain?" cried

Noddypoll.

The pirates stared at the sleeping snake.

"I think *that's* the Captain," whispered

Nong, pointing to the bulge in the

python's middle.

"Well, shiver me timbers!" said Noodle.

Then suddenly Nong began to cheer.

"Now there's no one to shout at us!"
he cried.

"There's no one to feed us to the sharks!"
shouted Noddypoll.

"There's no one to stop us going home!"
called Noodle.

The three pirates jumped for joy.

"First let's send Captain Pepper's pet
back where it came from," said Nong.
The pirates pulled back the hammock –
HEAVE!

And let it go –
TWANNNNNG!

The python flew through the air –

WHEEE! – and back into the jungle.

"HOORAY!" shouted the pirates.
And they danced a merry dance all
round the deck.

Chapter Six

Noddypoll, Noodle and Nong sailed
back across the sparkling seas until at
last they arrived home.

The three pirates sold the *Snooty Fox*
for a fortune, and bought
a tea shop instead.

On a perch in the
tea shop window sat
a parrot, to welcome
all the visitors.

As for Captain Pepper, his wish came true.

He soon became famous all over the world.

Captain Pepper was the only pirate in history to have been swallowed by his pet!

About the Author and Illustrator

Sally Grindley is an award-winning author, and pirates are some of her favourite characters. "I like writing about pirates because you can make them as silly as you like," she says. "And the crew in this story are definitely as silly as any I have ever met!" Sally Grindley's other books for Kingfisher include *The Giant Postman*, *What Are Friends For?*, *What Will I Do Without You?* and *Will You Forgive Me?*

David Parkins has illustrated lots of books for children, and is also the artist behind the *Beano*'s Dennis the Menace. "I love being an illustrator," he says, "but running a tea shop sounds fun, too. I'd find it difficult to resist all the cakes, though - especially the treacle tarts!"

Here are some more **I Am Reading** books for you to enjoy:

ALBERT'S RACCOON
Karen Wallace & Graham Percy

ALLIGATOR TAILS AND CROCODILE CAKES
Nicola Moon & Andy Ellis

BARN PARTY
Claire O'Brien & Tim Archbold

THE GIANT POSTMAN
Sally Grindley & Wendy Smith

GRANDAD'S DINOSAUR
Brough Girling & Stephen Dell

JJ RABBIT AND THE MONSTER
Nicola Moon & Ant Parker

JOE LION'S BIG BOOTS
Kara May & Jonathan Allen

JUST MABEL
Frieda Wishinsky & Sue Heap

KIT'S CASTLE
Chris Powling & Anthony Lewis

MISS WIRE AND THE THREE KIND MICE
Ian Whybrow & Emma Chichester Clark

MR COOL
Jacqueline Wilson & Stephen Lewis

MRS HIPPO'S PIZZA PARLOUR
Vivian French & Clive Scruton

PRINCESS ROSA'S WINTER
Judy Hindley & Margaret Chamberlain

RICKY'S RAT GANG
Anthony Masters & Chris Fisher

WATCH OUT, WILLIAM
Kady MacDonald Denton